THE PRESIDENT EXPRESS

BY **LIN OLIVER**   ILLUSTRATED BY **CHARLES S. PYLE**

GREAT RAILWAY ADVENTURES
SERIES 1 • ADVENTURE 2
Learning Curve Publishing
Chicago

LIONEL
AMERICAN LEGEND

For Laura and David Updegrove . . .
great pals of mine — L.O.

To Tina, for her patience, and the
California State Rail Museum, for their
invaluable assistance — C.P.

THE GREAT RAILWAY ADVENTURES BOOKS ARE IN MEMORY OF
MURRAY SCHRAMM, GREAT FRIEND AND MENTOR.

Library of Congress Catalog Card Number: 98-85456

ISBN 1-890647-51-9 (hardbound)
ISBN 1-890647-54-3 (paperback)

10 9 8 7 6 5 4 3 2 1

Special thanks to Taylor Bruce and Craig Marshall, the train crew who artfully
added color to this story. — C.P.

Text set in 14-point Simoncini Garamond
Art direction and text design by Joy Chu

Printed in the United States of America

It was no wonder that the Chicago Union Train Station was known as the Crossroads of the Nation.
With rows and rows of busy tracks, it was large enough to hold ten football fields.

Tuck and Billie Holden pressed their faces against the window as their train chugged into the grand station. They couldn't believe their eyes. Compared to the dusty little station in their California hometown, this looked like a palace.

A porter stuck his head in the door of Tuck and Billie's compartment.

"If you're planning to get out, make it quick," he said. "We leave for New York in exactly eighteen minutes."

"I don't think we should leave the train," Billie said to Tuck. "This station is so big, we may never find our way back."

"Stick with me," said Tuck. "I could find my way back from the moon."

Billie loved the way Tuck was always so sure of everything. He had taken good care of them since they set out on their journey two days before. With nothing more than his usual confidence, he had gotten them all the way across the country to Chicago. Now they were only nineteen hours from New York, where they hoped to surprise their parents at the World's Fair.

Tuck, Billie, and Chief wandered around the bustling Chicago station. People ran to catch trains while others bought spicy sausages from a hot-dog cart. There was even a magician to entertain the waiting passengers.

"Where are you kids from?" asked the magician, as he pulled the queen of hearts from a woman's ear.

"A small town in California," answered Tuck.

"If it's such a small town," said the magician, "I don't suppose there are many folks who can do this."

He waved a wand over his top hat and pulled out a rabbit.

Everyone in the crowd applauded — everyone, that is, but Chief.

When Chief saw the rabbit, he shot out of Billie's arms and bounded over to the magician. His tail wagged so hard that if it had been a propeller, he would have taken off into the air.

"What's with your dog?" yelled the magician.

"He just wants to play," said Billie. "He likes rabbits."

Unfortunately, the rabbit didn't feel the same way about Chief. Faster than you could say *abracadabra*, the rabbit leaped from the magician's hands and dashed across the station. Chief took off after him. Everyone else took off after Chief.

Around the station they all ran—through the restaurant, under the ticket counter, across the waiting rooms, up and down the grand concourse, and into the barbershop.

The rabbit hopped over a bald man in the barber chair and jumped into a drawer filled with combs and brushes. Chief followed right behind.

The magician burst into the barbershop screaming, "Don't hurt my rabbit!"

Chief didn't. In fact, he licked the little rabbit smack on the nose. Everyone laughed, even the magician.

The loudspeaker crackled, and a voice announced: "Train 409 for New York, departing on Track Four."

Tuck and Billie had been so busy trying to catch Chief that they hadn't noticed the time.

"Oh, no!" Tuck turned to Billie. "That's us."

They grabbed Chief and bolted for the train. When they got to Track Four, their train was already pulling out. Tuck and Billie raced along the platform, but they could not catch up. They watched as the train sped off into the distance.

Billie started to cry. Tuck put his arm around his sister.

"Don't be sad," he said. "I'll think of something."

Maynard Henry was standing nearby. He was a kindly man who hated to see a child cry.

"Those are some big tears for a little face," he said to Billie. "What's wrong?"

Tuck poured out their story. Their parents were at the New York World's Fair competing in the Invention of Tomorrow contest. He and Billie were supposed to stay back in California, but when they saved the life of a famous movie star, she gave them round-trip tickets to New York as a reward. Now they were on their way to surprise their parents.

"But we missed our train," added Billie. "We'll never get there."

"*Never* is a mighty big word," said Mr. Henry, "and one I don't happen to believe in."

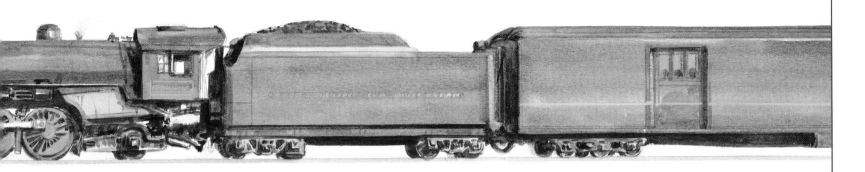

Mr. Henry pointed to a shining green engine on the next track.

"That's the *President Washington*," he said. "One of twenty powerful engines named after American presidents. I'm the engineer of that fine locomotive." Mr. Henry's eyes shone with pride. "A lot of folks told me I would never become an engineer," he went on, "but I believe there's always a way to do what you really want to do."

"We want to reach our parents," said Tuck. "The contest starts tomorrow morning, and more than anything, Billie and I want to be there with them."

Mr. Henry could feel how much Tuck and Billie loved their parents.

"I'm heading out for Washington, D.C.," he said. "If you ride there with me, I'll get you a lift on the overnight train into New York."

"You would do that for us?" asked Tuck.

"You children have lots of heart," Mr. Henry smiled, "and that goes a long way with me."

A few minutes later, Tuck and Billie were sitting next to Mr. Henry in the cab of the *President Washington*. When the all-clear signal was flashed, he opened up the throttle and the engine let out a burst of steam.

Womph . . . womph . . . womph! The thumping of the locomotive rose up loud and strong. Tuck and Billie could feel its vibrations in their bones. Slowly, the mighty train began to move, passing long freight trains lined up in the yard. Clickity-clack went the wheels as the *President Washington Express* gathered up speed and headed east.

It wasn't long before they were in open country.

"So your parents are inventors," Mr. Henry said. "What exactly did they invent?"

"The Dome Car," answered Tuck. "It's a train car made of glass. When you ride in it, you can see all around. It was my idea."

"Where does a whippersnapper like you get a fine idea like that?" said Mr. Henry.

"Do you really like it?" asked Tuck.

"I certainly do." Mr. Henry smiled. "Many a time I've crossed this beautiful land of ours wishing I had eyes in the back of my head so I could see everything around me." He reached out and shook Tuck's hand. "I'd be real proud if someday you'd invite me to take a ride on your Dome Car."

"You'll be the first passenger," said Tuck. "I promise."

By the time the *President Washington* crossed into Pennsylvania, huge rain clouds covered the sky.

"Looks like we're in for some weather," Mr. Henry said.

The rain came soon, pouring down in thick sheets of water. Thunder echoed over the hills. Bolts of lightning flashed across the sky.

Tuck and Billie had never seen anything like it. Storms in California were mild and passed quickly. There was something about this weather that felt wild.

As the *President Washington* wound its way into the mountains, a huge bolt of lightning lit up the whole sky.

"Gee whiz," said Tuck. "Look at that!"

Mr. Henry wasn't looking at the sky. His eyes were focused on the entrance of the tunnel

up ahead, an underground passage known to trainmen as the Horseshoe. He didn't like what he saw.

"The signal is out," he said. "The lightning must have hit it."

Billie and Tuck swallowed hard. They knew that without a working signal, it was dangerous to enter the tunnel. They would have no way to tell if another train was coming in the opposite direction.

Mr. Henry pulled the train to a stop at the entrance of the Horseshoe. The conductor came into the cab, carrying a fat train schedule under his arm.

"A freight train out of West Virginia was supposed to have come through the Horseshoe over an hour ago," he said. "Nothing else on the schedule. We should be clear to go."

The conductor left and Mr. Henry took a deep breath. Then he took hold of the throttle and ever so carefully eased the *President Washington* into the Horseshoe.

It was pitch black inside. The train inched along. Suddenly, there was a rumbling noise.

"I hope that's just thunder," said Billie.

"I can't tell," said Mr. Henry. "It could be a train coming around the horseshoe turn."

"The conductor said no trains were scheduled," said Tuck.

"Unless the storm made that freight train late," said Mr. Henry. "If that's the case, we're in for a heap of trouble."

He grabbed the lantern and hopped out of the engine. The ground was slippery and Mr. Henry's foot slid out from under him. He fell down hard.

Tuck and Billie jumped from the engine.

"Mr. Henry!" they shouted. "Are you hurt?"

Mr. Henry couldn't get up. "My ankle," he said. "It's twisted. I can't walk."

Tuck put his ear down on the track. He heard a rumble coming from deep underground.

"That's not thunder," he said. "There's another train in this tunnel."

"I've got to warn them we're here," said Mr. Henry, struggling to stand up. "Unless they stop, we're in for a crash!"

They had to move quickly, but Mr. Henry was hurt and could barely walk. Tuck took the lantern and stood up. Billie took hold of his arm. They knew what they had to do.

Clutching the lantern, Tuck ran down the track as fast as he could with Billie close behind. When they rounded the horseshoe turn, they stopped short. Coming right toward them was the freight train!

Tuck planted his feet and raised the lantern. He waved it back and forth, hoping the engineer would see his signal.

The headlights from the freight train came closer and closer. Tuck and Billie held their breath. Over the roar of the train, they could barely make out a small voice in the distance.

"There's a signal to stop," the voice called.

The next thing Tuck and Billie heard was the screech of brakes echoing throughout the tunnel. The freight train lurched to a stop just ten feet in front of them.

A moment later, Mr. Henry rounded the turn. "Good job, whippersnappers." He beamed with relief. "Like I said, you kids got a lot of heart."

Hours later, when Mr. Henry pulled the train into Washington, D.C., word had already spread of the near accident in the tunnel. A crowd had gathered to welcome the *President Washington* safely home.

As Tuck and Billie helped Mr. Henry off the train, a man waving a gold-handled walking stick stepped up to them.

"My name is Thaddeus Winterbottom," he said, "and I am the president of the railroad. I came here to congratulate you on your bravery."

"This is quite an honor, sir," said Tuck.

"The honor is mine," said Mr. Winterbottom. "To express my gratitude, I'd like to invite you youngsters to be the first passengers on the *Torpedo*, the Locomotive of Tomorrow. She makes her first run into New York City tonight. Would you like to ride along?"

"You bet," said Tuck. "We've been trying to get to the World's Fair to meet our parents."

"Then you shall get there in style," smiled Mr. Winterbottom. He turned to Mr. Henry. "And as for you, sir," he said, "I'd be honored if you would serve as the engineer of the *Torpedo*. You are the railroad's finest."

Maynard Henry's eyes filled with tears. He had waited a long time for this moment.

Tuck and Billie were shown into the back seat of Mr. Winterbottom's big car. As they settled into the comfortable seats, their thoughts turned to their amazing railway adventure. Just days before, they had been at home in San Luis Obispo, California. Tomorrow, they would enter New York City on the fastest locomotive in the world. They would get to see the Dome Car in the Invention of Tomorrow contest, and best of all, their family would be together again.

Tuck and Billie smiled happily. Tomorrow was going to be a very good day.

THE PRESIDENT EXPRESS

The next time you take a train trip or play with your model trains, you can use some of these train terms that have been handed down over the years.

TRAIN TALK

BRAKEMAN The person responsible for the brakes working correctly. The brakeman checks the brakes throughout the train trip. On passenger trains, he assists the conductor.

CABOOSE The caboose is also called the cabin car, hack, or crummy. It is usually the last car on a freight train. The conductor and crew eat, work, and sleep in the caboose.

CONDUCTOR On a freight train, the conductor is called the skipper. He is the boss.

COW CATCHER This metal bumper or grate was first put on the front of engines in the 1830s. It helped push cattle, buffalo, and rocks off the train tracks.

DISPATCHER A dispatcher works in the train yard coordinating arrivals and departures by assigning each train to move ahead, meet, pass, and arrive on a certain track.

DUMP THE AIR Railroaders' slang for putting on the emergency brakes.

ENGINEER The engineer drives the train. He is also called the hogger.

FIREMAN On the old steam trains, the fireman shoveled coal into the firebox. He could look at the color of the burning fire and know whether it was the correct temperature.

HIGHBALL A favorite word of train crews, meaning that the track is clear and the train can go full speed ahead. Railroaders also use this term to describe going fast: "Let's highball."

SIGNALS Train crews can use their hands or flags by day and lanterns at night to give commands. For example, a lantern swung across the track tells the train to stop.

WINDOW MUSIC Railroaders' slang for the passing scenery. "Sit back and enjoy the window music."

IF YOU WANT TO LEARN MORE ABOUT TRAINS, ASK YOUR LIBRARIAN FOR SUGGESTIONS. THERE ARE MANY WONDERFUL BOOKS ON TRAIN TRAVEL, THE HISTORY OF TRAINS, AND MODEL TRAINS.

The President *engines were built for the Baltimore and Ohio Railroad, and all used the names of American presidents. The engines were olive green with gold and maroon trim.*